I CAN READ ABOUT
CREEPY CRAWLY CREATURES

Written by C. J. Naden

Illustrated by Jean Chandler

Troll Associates

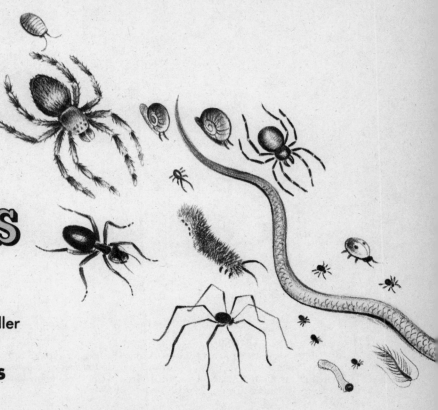

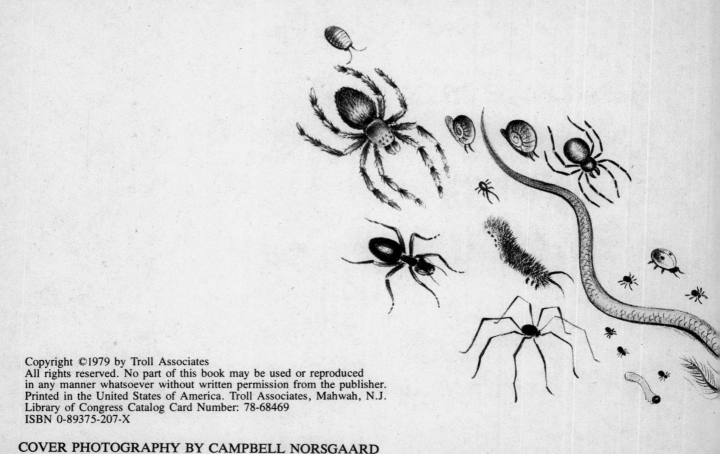

COVER PHOTOGRAPHY BY CAMPBELL NORSGAARD

Here they come!

They creep and crawl and squiggle and scrunch. They
wiggle and wobble and slither and slink. They are ants
and bugs and caterpillars and centipedes and lizards and snails
and snakes and spiders and worms. They are the creepy, crawly
creatures. And they are everywhere!

Lift a rock, and there's a worm.
Walk in tall grass, and there's a snake.

Stand under a tree, and there's a fuzzy
caterpillar dropping down.

It's a creepy, crawly invasion!

They may make you shiver, but you should not
be afraid. Creepy, crawly creatures are some
of the most fascinating things in the
animal kingdom.

SNAKE

LIZARD

SNAIL

Some creepy, crawly creatures are insects like ants and fleas.
Some creepy, crawly creatures are reptiles like lizards and snakes.
Some creepy, crawly creatures are snails with shells.

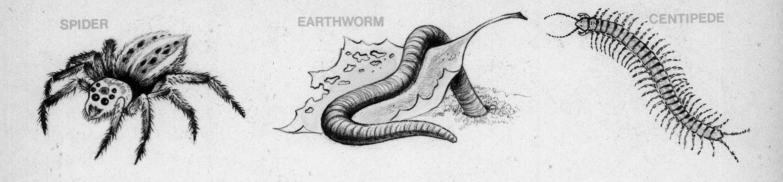

SPIDER   EARTHWORM   CENTIPEDE

Other creepy crawlers are spiders, and earthworms and centipedes. They creep and they crawl and they live in a very fascinating world.

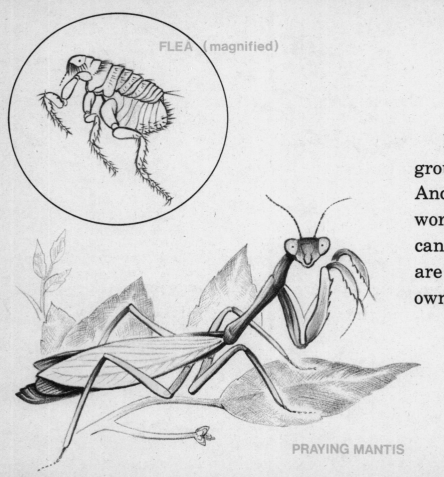

FLEA (magnified)

PRAYING MANTIS

Insects belong to the largest group of animals in the world. And they live everywhere in the world. Some are so small you can hardly see them. Others are like giants in their own world.

No matter what size or shape or color, it's easy to tell an insect. All adult insects have six legs. They have three legs on each side of their bodies.

A spider has eight legs, so you know it is not an insect.

An insect's body has three main parts — the head, the thorax, and the abdomen.

If it doesn't have three parts, it isn't an insect. How many parts does the spider's body have?

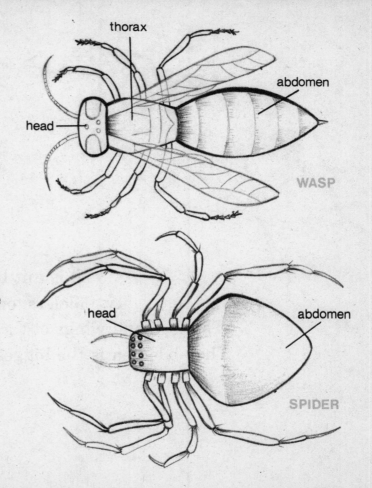

thorax

head

abdomen

WASP

head

abdomen

SPIDER

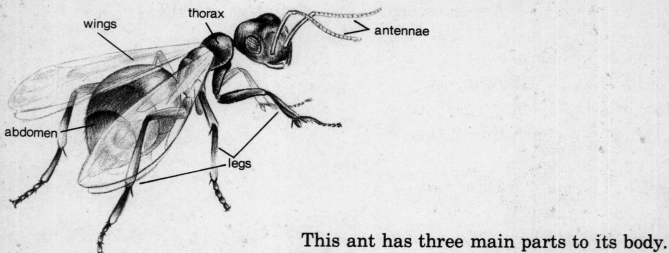

wings

thorax

antennae

abdomen

legs

This ant has three main parts to its body.
Two feelers, or *antennae*, grow out of its head.
The legs and wings of the ant are attached to the thorax.
The abdomen is the biggest part. It contains the stomach.

Are the scorpion and centipede insects?

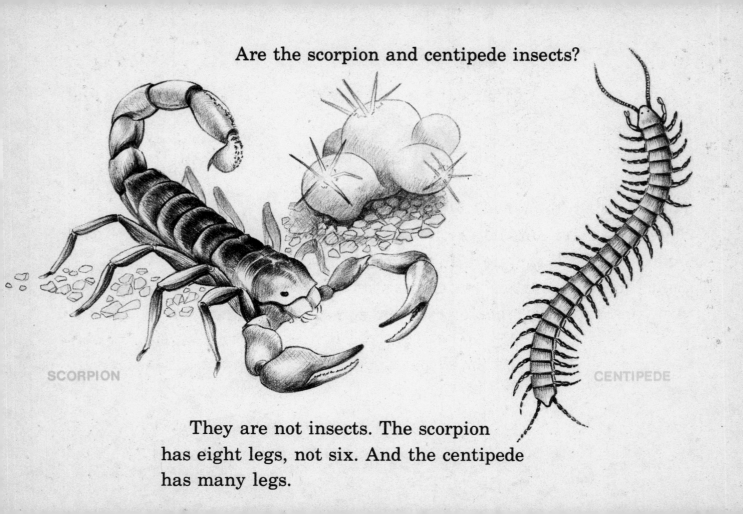

SCORPION

CENTIPEDE

They are not insects. The scorpion
has eight legs, not six. And the centipede
has many legs.

Ants seem to be everywhere.

There are more ants on earth than any other kind of insect.

Scientists think there are 15,000 different kinds of ants.

Some ants are meat-eaters. Some ants eat seeds. Some eat honey.

Ants are brown or black or red, and sometimes yellow.

Ants live in groups called colonies.
Thousands of ants may live in one
colony. Each ant in the colony
has a job to do. There are
three different kinds of ants
in a colony — the worker ants,
the male ants, and the queen ants.

A queen ant spends her
life laying eggs. Sometimes a
colony has only one queen, but
sometimes there are more. The
queen can live as long as
15 years.

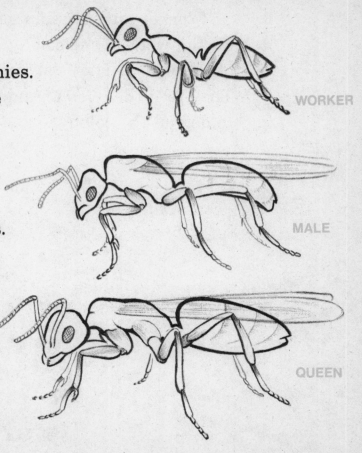

WORKER

MALE

QUEEN

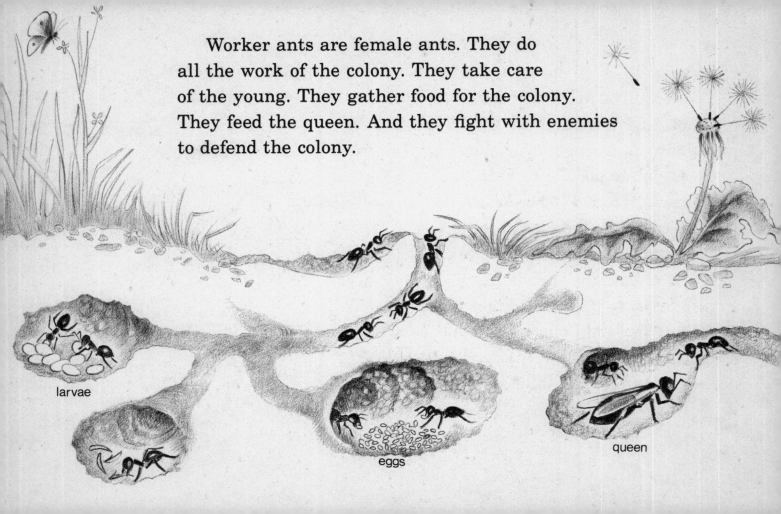

Worker ants are female ants. They do
all the work of the colony. They take care
of the young. They gather food for the colony.
They feed the queen. And they fight with enemies
to defend the colony.

larvae

eggs

queen

Worker ants can live as long as five years.
The job of the male ants is to mate with the queens.
Soon after mating, they die.

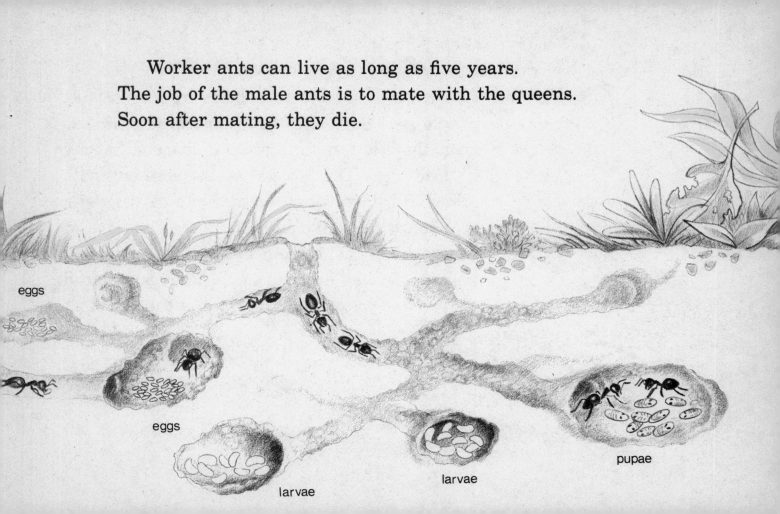

eggs

eggs

larvae

larvae

pupae

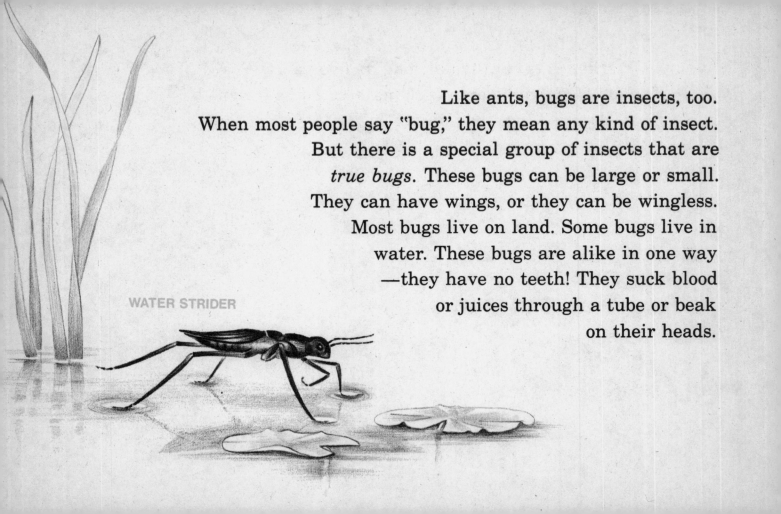

WATER STRIDER

Like ants, bugs are insects, too.
When most people say "bug," they mean any kind of insect.
But there is a special group of insects that are
true bugs. These bugs can be large or small.
They can have wings, or they can be wingless.
Most bugs live on land. Some bugs live in
water. These bugs are alike in one way
—they have no teeth! They suck blood
or juices through a tube or beak
on their heads.

Water bugs and bedbugs
and stinkbugs are
all bugs. But
potato bugs and
June bugs are not
bugs at all. They
are beetles.

Most bugs are harmless...
which is a good thing ... because
there are so many of them.

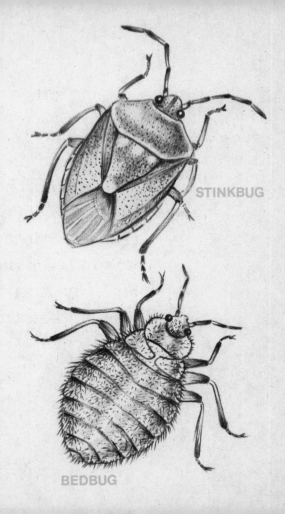

STINKBUG

BEDBUG

The crawly caterpillar looks
something like a worm, but it is
not a worm. The caterpillar
is the *larva* of a butterfly
or moth. It is on its
way to becoming a
butterfly. As a larva,
it is in its second stage
of growth.

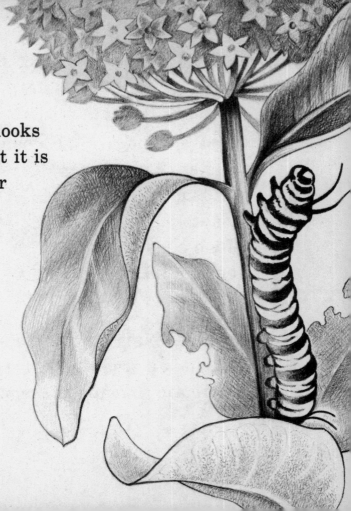

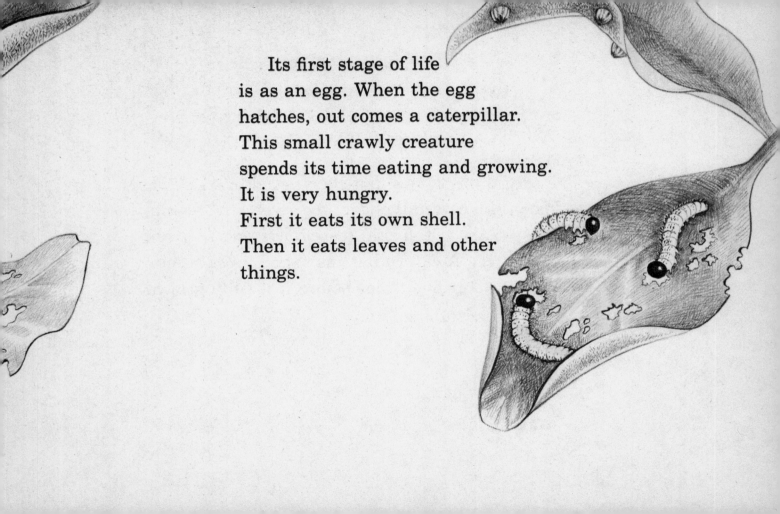

Its first stage of life
is as an egg. When the egg
hatches, out comes a caterpillar.
This small crawly creature
spends its time eating and growing.
It is very hungry.
First it eats its own shell.
Then it eats leaves and other
things.

The caterpillar grows, but its outer skin does not.
When the caterpillar gets too large for its skin,
the skin just cracks and falls off.
A caterpillar may shed its skin four
or five times before it is fully grown.

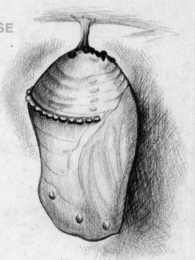

When the caterpillar is grown,
it goes on to the next stage of its
life. The caterpillar finds a leaf
or twig, and forms a case or a cocoon
around itself. It is now called a pupa.

The pupa grows inside the cocoon.
Some take all winter to grow. Others
take as long as eight months to grow.

But, in the end, the crawly caterpillar is gone, and out comes a beautiful, fluttering butterfly.

Instead of crawling like a caterpillar,
the lizard slithers along on its four legs.
A lizard is a reptile, like a snake.
Reptiles are cold-blooded animals.
Their bodies stay the same temperature as the
outside temperature. Most lizards live
in warm places.

KOMODO DRAGON

Lizards come in all sizes and shapes.
There are about 3,000 different kinds of lizards
in the world.

Some are very tiny and grow only a few centimeters long. Some lizards look like snakes with legs. Others are very large and look almost like crocodiles.

The biggest lizard is called the dragon of Komodo. It lives in the East Indies, and it grows about 10 feet, or 3 meters, long. The Komodo lizard is a giant creepy crawler.

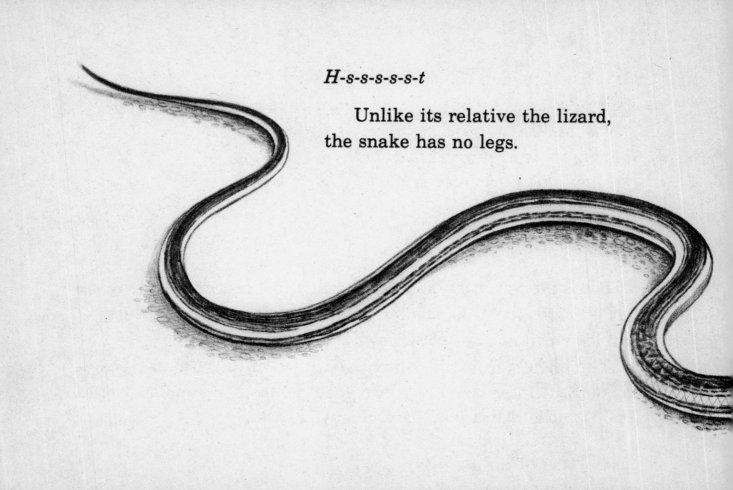

H-s-s-s-s-t

Unlike its relative the lizard,
the snake has no legs.

It crawls along by wriggling its slender body.
The snake's backbone is a long chain of about 300 tiny bones.
So the snake can bend easily, as it slithers across
the ground in a curving motion.

CORAL SNAKE

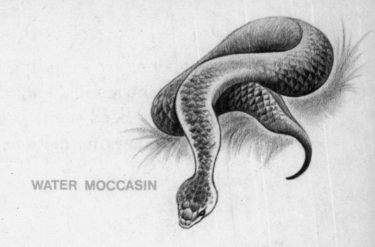

WATER MOCCASIN

RATTLESNAKE

There are almost as many kinds of snakes as there are lizards. Some people are afraid of snakes. But only a few snakes are dangerous. Rattlesnakes and water moccasins and coral snakes are poisonous.

One of the most interesting things about snakes
is the way they eat. They swallow their food whole.
A large python can swallow an animal that weighs about
100 pounds, or 45 kilograms. Strong juices in the snake's stomach
will digest the animal—everything but the feathers or hair!

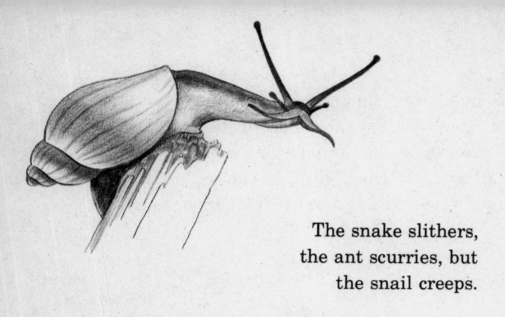

The snake slithers,
the ant scurries, but
the snail creeps.

Snails belong to the class of animals
called gastropods (GAS-tra-pods). This word comes
from a word that means "belly-footed creatures."
   The snail creeps along on a
muscle that is called a "foot."
When the muscle pushes backward,
it makes the snail move forward.
   The snail has a soft
body covered by a
hard shell.

There are thousands of different kinds of snails. Some live on land; some live in the sea; and some live in fresh water.

Some snails are so tiny you cannot see them. Some grow as long as two feet, or 61 centimeters.

Most snails feed on plants.

The crawly spider feeds on insects like flies and mosquitoes. Some big spiders eat lizards or birds. Some spiders eat each other. The female spider will often eat the smaller male.

A spider is not an insect.

It belongs to a group
called the arachnids (a-RACK-nids).

PEDIPALPS
(MOUTH PARTS)

A spider does not have wings or antennae. But it does have a two-part body with eight legs, and two mouth parts up front. Most spiders are small. But the tarantula can grow as large as a person's hand.

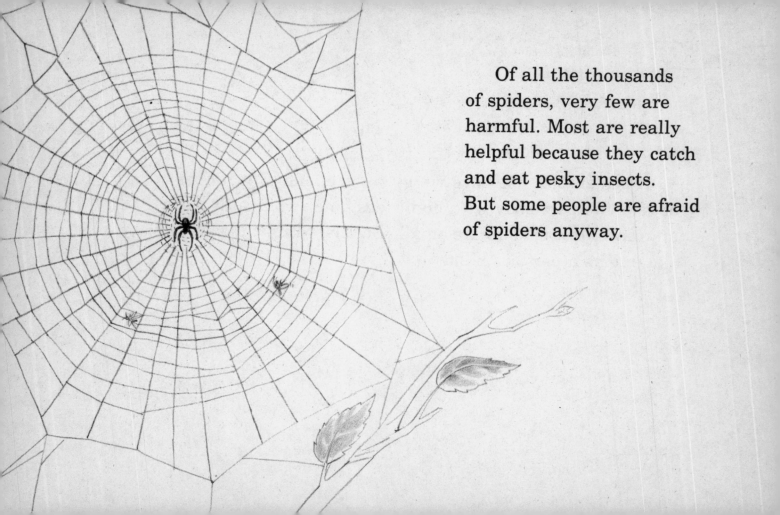

Of all the thousands of spiders, very few are harmful. Most are really helpful because they catch and eat pesky insects. But some people are afraid of spiders anyway.

One of the most feared spiders
is the black widow. It is a poisonous
spider. The black widow has a red or
yellow patch on its abdomen.

One of the most interesting spiders
is the trap-door spider. It lives
underground and has a trap door to
the entrance of its home.

TRAP-DOOR
SPIDER

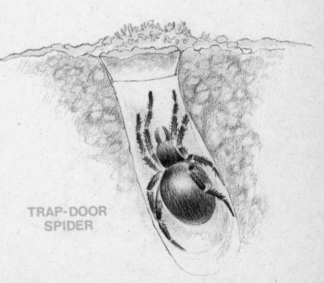

Spiders are best known for spinning silky
webs. All spiders spin silk, but not all make webs.
Most spiders spin webs to catch insects.
The silk is sticky. When an insect steps into
the web, it gets caught and cannot escape.
Then the spider crawls over the web
and eats its dinner.

The spider uses its eight legs to crawl across its web. But the earthworm has no legs at all. This creepy crawly creature tunnels underground most of the time. How does it move? The earthworm uses two sets of muscles to move along. One set pushes its body out, the other set pulls it up close together. In this way, the earthworm moves along.

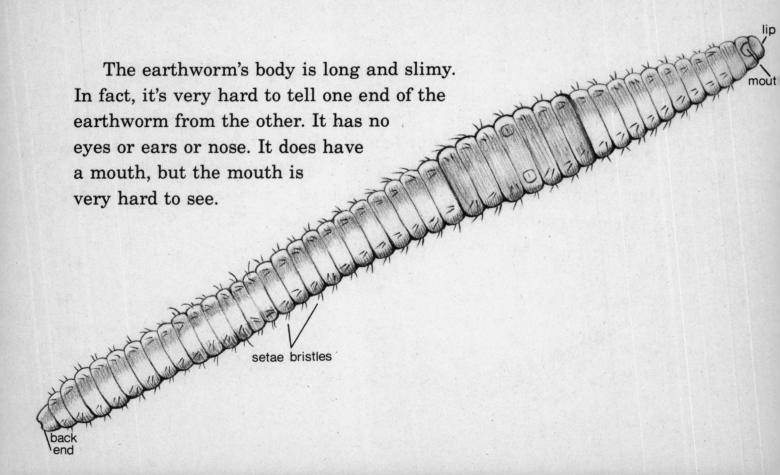

The earthworm's body is long and slimy. In fact, it's very hard to tell one end of the earthworm from the other. It has no eyes or ears or nose. It does have a mouth, but the mouth is very hard to see.

lip

mout

setae bristles

back
end

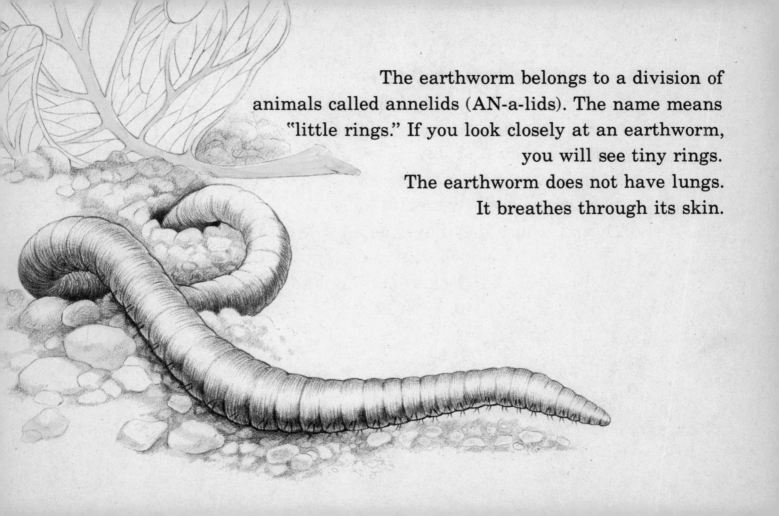

The earthworm belongs to a division of animals called annelids (AN-a-lids). The name means "little rings." If you look closely at an earthworm, you will see tiny rings. The earthworm does not have lungs. It breathes through its skin.

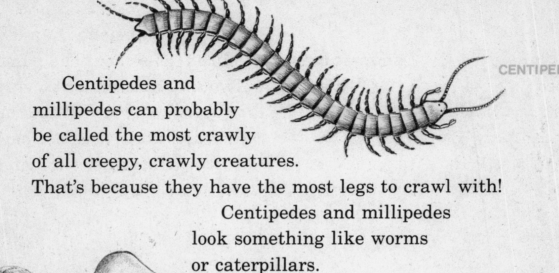

Centipedes and
millipedes can probably
be called the most crawly
of all creepy, crawly creatures.
That's because they have the most legs to crawl with!
Centipedes and millipedes
look something like worms
or caterpillars.

Centipede means "hundreds of feet or legs."
Millipede means "thousands of feet or legs."
The centipede has a flattened body. The millipede has
a rounded body. The centipede has two pairs of jaws,
and feelers. It eats worms and insects.
The millipede eats decayed plants.

MILLIPEDE

There are many things to discover
in the world around you.

From now on, perhaps you will want to
carefully watch where you walk.
There on a twig,
        or under a rock,
            or munching on a piece of grass
may be something very special
—one of the world's marvelous creepy,
crawly creatures.